EMMA
IS ON THE AIR
#2: PARTY DRAMA!

by IDA SIEGAL

illustrations by
KARLA PEÑA

SCHOLASTIC PRESS/NEW YORK

CONTENTS

CHAPTER ONE

Festival News

READY, Sophia?"

"Yup, ready, Emma!"

"One, two, THREE! Woo-hoo!!!" Sophia and I screamed and laughed as we slid head-first into a huge pile of leaves in the school yard.

"Ha-ha! That was so fun!" shouted Sophia. She stood up and began brushing all the red, orange, and yellow leaves off her coat. I was still buried under the pile.

"Emma?" Sophia called out as she looked around. I waited silently as Sophia searched for me.

"Emma?" she asked again. "Where are you?"

Then I leapt out of the leaf pile!

"Roar!" I yelled like a lion.

"Ahhh!" she screamed as leaves flew everywhere around us. Then we both fell back down laughing.

"Emma, your hair!" Sophia pointed. "You look like a wicked autumn witch!"

I felt the top of my head and realized I had leaves stuck in between all my long chocolate-pudding Slinkies. You know, my curly hair.

"That's because I *am* a wicked autumn witch!" I giggled. Then I held up my arms like a zombie and pretended I was going to stomp on Sophia. She ran away, screaming so loud a bunch

of other kids in the school yard heard and ran over to play with us.

"Look out below!" called Javier as he dove into the leaf pile like a cannonball. Leaves were flying everywhere.

We bounced and ran and danced in the leaves until Carmen the yard monitor said it was time to come inside.

"Okay, class, settle down," said Miss Thompson as we walked into our classroom. "Take out your Spanish workbooks and turn to page thirty-one."

I love doing Spanish in school. I know lots of the answers because we speak Spanish at home. Spanish is a very famous language, you know. I feel extra famous showing off my Spanish speaking skills!

I have lots of reasons to feel famous these days. After I solved the mystery of Javier's wormburger at school last month, everyone started coming to me for help. They wanted me to do news reports on them, too.

Like when my friend Shakira lost her sister's gold heart necklace, I did an investigation and discovered it fell behind the couch in her living room. After I did my news report, Shakira's mom looked behind the sofa and found the necklace! She found an old magazine, too! Bonus.

And at school, my friend David only had two cookies at lunch one day even though his mom always packs four. I used my camera phone to shoot video of cookie crumbs on Adrian's hoodie sweatshirt. I showed Adrian the evidence and he sang like a canary! (That means he admitted to stealing the cookies, in detective language.)

"¿Quién quiere leer?" asked Miss Thompson in *Spanish* language. "Who wants to read . . . ?" Then she paused when she saw my hair. "Emma, what happened to your hair? Leaves are stuck everywhere," she said with a concerned smile.

"I know!" I smiled back. "I like it this way. I'm a wicked autumn witch!"

"Oh, I see. Actually, that reminds me," she added, turning to the rest of the class. "Before we begin our Spanish lesson, I have an important announcement to make. As you know, Halloween is coming up soon . . ."

We all started oohing and giggling with excitement.

"Yes, yes," Miss Thompson continued, "and as you also know, the Washington Heights

Halloween Festival will be held at our school next Saturday. But this year, in addition to games, a bounce house, and the Halloween dance . . . there's also going to be a costume contest!"

The whole class started oohing and aahing even louder. This was big news.

"Yes, it will be lots of fun," she went on. "Students from all the neighborhood schools will be competing in different categories, like most original costume. Or best group costume. Funniest costume! We want to show our P.S. 387 pride! Principal Lee says the class that wins the most categories will get a pizza party the following week!"

We all screamed and shouted!!

"Okay, okay, settle down. There are some rules you need to know about. First, you have to try to *make* your costume yourself. Your friends and family can help. And second, all costumes should be based on a literary character."

"Ooooh!" we all shrieked.

"Miss Thompson, what's a literary character?" asked Javier.

"I'm glad you asked that, Javier. A literary character is a character from a book. So I want you to think hard about the characters in your favorite books and pick which one you want to dress up as for the Halloween costume contest."

Ooh. Yes! A great costume idea popped right into my brain. But I was gonna need some help.

CHAPTER TWO

Wear What You Want!

AFTER school, everyone was talking about their Halloween costumes.

Lizzie decided to be Dorothy from *The Wizard of Oz*. And Miss Thompson said that counts because *The Wizard of Oz* is a movie *and* a book!

Shakira said she would be Charlotte the spider from *Charlotte's Web*.

Adrian wanted to be a Wild Thing from *Where the Wild Things Are*. We all laughed because he's pretty wild even when it isn't Halloween.

Molly wanted to be Roo, the kid kangaroo from *Winnie-the-Pooh*, but when we were all waiting for the bus after school, Melissa G. told her she couldn't.

"But I like Roo," Molly replied. She sounded sad and a little embarrassed.

"But Molly, my three-year-old baby cousin is dressing up as Piglet from *Winnie-the-Pooh*. Everybody knows *Winnie-the-Pooh* costumes are baby costumes. I'm just trying to help you. Do you want people to call you a baby on Halloween?"

"I guess not," Molly answered with a frown. Melissa G. and Molly are perfect-match friends. Just like me and Sophia. Only me and Sophia are nice to each other. Melissa G. says not-nice things to Molly all the time. It's not right.

So I walked over to them and said, "Let her wear what she wants, Melissa!"

Melissa G. scowled at me. "Mind your own business, Emma!"

Melissa G. has been mean to me ever since I became a news reporter. That's because people stopped caring that she was in a toothpaste commercial. She hates that I'm more famous than she is.

"Whatever, Melissa," I said back. Then I looked at Molly and said, "I like Roo and I like *Winnie-the-Pooh*. You should be whatever you want for Halloween." I turned back to Melissa G. and said, "So there." And I stuck my tongue out at her. Then she stuck her tongue out at me.

Sophia saw us arguing and walked over. "I like *Winnie-the-Pooh*, too," she said in a nice voice.

"That's okay, Sophia," Molly said. "Melissa's right—it's kind of babyish. I'll think of something else."

Sophia and I shrugged our shoulders and got into line to get on the bus. Molly really should stand up to Melissa G., but we couldn't make her if she didn't want to.

"I have the PERFECT costume!!" I told Sophia as we sat down in our usual seats on the bus.

"Ooh, what is it?" she asked.

"Well, it's from a book the fourth graders are reading in class!" I said.

"Oh, wow. What book is it?" Sophia wanted to know.

"It's called *The Lion, the Witch, and the Wardrobe*," I told her.

"Oh!! I know that book! My older sister, Olivia, has it in her room. It looks sooo good."

"Yup! I'll be the Witch... see, I kind of already am!" I pointed to my pudding Slinkies, still covered in leaves. "I just need someone to be the Lion and someone else to be the wardrobe... and we are guaranteed to win the costume contest!"

"That's so cool. I'll be the Lion!" Sophia offered.

"Great! Now we just need someone to dress up as the wardrobe."

Sophia and I started looking around the bus. We spotted Javier sitting in the back. He looked like he was pretending the bus was a spaceship and he was preparing to land on the moon.

Ever since I solved Javier's wormburger mystery, he's kind of become our friend. Actually, Javier volunteers to help me sometimes.

Like when I had to find Shakira's sister's missing gold heart necklace, Javier was the one who suggested looking behind the sofa with a flashlight. He said one time he looked behind the sofa in his house and found his sister's ring! It was right next to a rubber band and a peanut-butter-and-jelly sandwich he was saving for later and forgot about. *Yuck.*

Javier also helped me figure out why there were never enough basketballs during free time at gym. He did some snooping and found six missing basketballs stuck in the back of the equipment closet. I did a news report on it, and then all the kids got to play basketball. Javier has good snooping skills, I must say.

We're actually like a reporting team. Sophia likes to hold the camera phone when we do interviews. She helps me think about clues. I ask the questions and do the news reports. And Javier searches for clues.

In fact, Javier has being doing such a good job snooping, we decided that he should have his own set of tools. Spy tools! Javier says he needs a flashlight (for looking behind things), a magnifying glass (for inspecting things), walkie-talkies (for telling us about things he found), and night-vision goggles (for seeing monsters in the dark, in case they decide to follow him while he snoops at night—I told Javier that sounded silly, but he said snooping detectives have to be prepared for anything).

The only problem is the spy kit costs money. Lots of money. We added up Sophia's allowance, my birthday money, and Javier's tooth-fairy money, but it's still not enough to buy the spy kit. It'll have to wait.

"Hey, Javier!" I called to him in the back of the bus. He was still making spaceship noises.

Apparently the school bus/spaceship was about to make a crash landing.

"Errr . . . oh, no . . . watch out, moon creature . . . we're comin' in!!" he said. After a few more *booms* and *pows*, Javier finally looked up.

"Oh, hey, Emma," he said.

"Javier, do you have a costume for the Halloween contest yet?" I asked.

"No. Not yet," he replied with a toothless smile. Javier barely has any teeth. His baby ones keep falling out and his grown-up ones haven't grown in yet.

"Wanna be a wardrobe for Halloween?" I asked. I hoped he would say yes, but I wasn't sure. He might think a wardrobe was a boring costume.

"Are you kidding? Of course YES!!" Javier stood up in his seat and held his arms in the air. I think he was excited.

"Perfect!" I squealed. "Now we have a Lion, a Witch, and a wardrobe!"

"But ... hey, Emma?" Javier interrupted. "What's a wardrobe?"

"Javier?! You agreed to be a wardrobe even though you don't know what it is?"

"Of course I did! You asked me to be a wardrobe. I knew it would be great—whatever it was."

Suddenly I felt a little embarrassed. Like good embarrassed. Like I was going to blush. Sometimes I wish everyone else knew that Javier is a really nice kid. People say he's weird, but that's because they don't know him. I think he's pretty smart! And funny, too.

"Javier, a wardrobe is like a closet," I explained. "But it's a closet that's a piece of furniture."

"I'm going to be a piece of furniture for Halloween?" Javier asked.

"Um . . . well . . . yeah, I was thinking . . ."

"That . . . is . . . the . . . coolest . . . costume EVER!" Javier straightened his body and pretended to be really stiff—just like furniture.

That settled that. Our costume group was all set and we were going to make the best costumes ever.

CHAPTER THREE

The Lion, the Witch, and the Wardrobe

HEY, Mom!" I shouted as I jumped off the school bus.

"Hi, honey!" she replied. "How was school today?"

"It was awesome!" I shouted. "You know what happened?"

"Nope. But I'm hoping you'll tell me." Mom smiled and checked to make sure my baby sister, Mia, was still asleep in the stroller.

"There's gonna be a costume contest at school and you have to make your own costume and it has to be from a book and I know what I'm gonna be and it's gonna be sooo cool," I said in a hurry. I had to stop to take a breath.

"Okay, Emma, slow down. And try not to yell, your sister's sleeping."

"Okay," I said in a whisper. "But, Mom," I continued in my normal voice, "I'm going to be a witch! But not just any witch. I'm going to be the Witch from *The Lion, the Witch, and the Wardrobe!*"

"Now that sounds wonderful, Emma. Very creative."

Mom told me that the Witch from *The Lion, the Witch, and the Wardrobe* is called the White Witch and she wears a long white fur coat and has a magic wand! They have all the supplies we need at the craft store. Mom said could we could go tomorrow morning since it was Saturday and there was no school.

The next morning, I nibbled on some bacon and eggs before we left for the craft store.

"So what do you think about my costume idea, Papi?" I asked my dad.

"I think it's wonderful," Papi replied. "You're going to be *la Bruja Blanca*!"

"Ha! I like it when you say "White Witch" in Spanish! It sounds so spooky!" I said it out loud like this: *"Brooha Blahnkah."*

"We'll make you a super-spooky costume."

"That's perfect! *Perfecto.*" I popped a forkful of scrambled eggs into my mouth.

"Meow, meow," my cat, Luna, chimed in as she jumped into my lap.

"You think so, too, Luna?" I asked as I

scrunched down to give her a kiss and a snuggle.

Luna has chocolate-pudding cat fur, just like my chocolate-pudding Slinky curls. She's also my reporter's assistant, so she's allowed to sit at the table even though Papi says he's not thrilled about it.

After breakfast, we all got in the car to go buy costume supplies.

"Wow," I said as we stepped inside the craft store.

"EEEK. GAGA GAGA," agreed baby Mia.

The store was huge! They had every kind of crafting supply, in every kind of color you could ever think of!

"Papi, this is amazing!"

"It is pretty cool," Papi replied.

We looked around for everything a witch could ever need. They had a ton of hats and

brooms and black fabric. They had glitter and feathers and beads. But I mostly just needed white stuff because I was going to be the White Witch.

After a while, I found a white sheet that Mom said we could cut up to make a witch's dress. We grabbed lots of white feathers and sequins to decorate my dress. Then I found the perfect magic wand—it was gold and shiny. Papi said the White Witch also has a crown. So we bought a package of tinfoil to make spiky icicles. We were going to attach them to a princess crown I already had at home.

Last, but not least, I needed a long white fur coat.

"Mom, I don't see any fur coats around here."

"Hmm. A white fur coat. Let's see," said Mom as she handed baby Mia over to Papi. Mia was getting fussy, so he took her back to the car for a bottle.

"I know, Emma," said Mom as an idea popped into her head.

"What?" I asked.

"How about this?" She held up a white shaggy rug.

"A rug? Do you think the White Witch would really wear a rug?"

"I sure do," Mom insisted. "Look, we'll get the medium size ... wrap it around the top like a cape ... and then cinch it around your waist. Then we'll cut holes for your arms. It'll be great."

I suddenly had a vision of myself in a white shaggy rug coat and it was amazing.

"Actually, that's kinda cool! Let's get it!" I agreed.

We left the craft store with everything we needed.

Mom, Papi, and I spent the next few days putting my costume together. Miss Thompson told us to bring our costumes into school a couple days before the festival so we could finish them up in art class. I brought all my witch stuff, plus a special surprise for Sophia to add to her Lion costume.

"Okay, class, it's time to grab your costumes and bring them to the art room," announced Miss Thompson. "Your art instructor, Mr. Colón, will help with the finishing touches. And one more thing: As you know, the costume contest will have prizes for all the different categories. The Halloween Festival organizers announced there will also be a grand prize for the best costume overall. It's a gift certificate to Mr. Magee's Toy Store."

We all squealed with excitement!!

"So if you win best costume," Miss Thompson continued, "you can pick out any toy you like, within reason, from Mr. Magee's."

"Sophia, we have to win now!!" I exclaimed as we walked to the art room. "Mr. Magee has a spy kit. I've seen it in the window. It'll be perfect for Javier!"

"*Ooh*, Emma, he would love that," Sophia

agreed. We sat down at a big brown table in the art room. It was covered in dried paint splats.

"Yes, we have to win. I think we can do it," Sophia continued. "Check out my costume. My mom says the Lion from *The Lion, the Witch, and the Wardrobe* is named Aslan and he is fierce. We spent hours making my Aslan costume fierce!"

"Ooh, Sophia, I love it!" I told her.

"See, look," Sophia said as she plopped her costume down on the table, "I have an orange leotard and tan tights. My mom helped me make a tan oval out of felt and sew it on the leotard for the Lion's stomach. Then we made a mane from strips of felt in yellow, orange, red, and tan! We made the strips into loops and glued them around a headband."

"It looks so real," I told her. "But not quite real enough . . ."

"What do mean it's not real enough?" Sophia sounded confused.

Then I pulled out my surprise for her. Luna's fur brush!

"Look!" I showed her. "We'll just take some of Luna's cat fur and paste it on your costume and then you'll be like a real lion!"

"Ooh, wow! This is perfect!" Sophia squealed.

She pasted Luna's fur onto the leotard in the shape of a semicircle near the neck. It looked better than I had imagined. There was no way we could lose.

"This is wonderful, Sophia!" said Mr. Colón, the art teacher, as he walked over to our table. "I love this colorful lion's mane. Very creative."

"Thanks, Mr. Colón." Sophia beamed.

"Nice costume, Sophia," said Melissa G. as she walked by our table.

I sighed.

"Thanks, Melissa," Sophia replied.

I just rolled my eyes because you could tell Melissa G. didn't really mean it when she said "nice costume." I knew she was jealous and probably worried we'd win the contest.

"Yeah, it looks awesome!" said Molly, who was walking behind Melissa G. "It really looks just like a lion. Good job, Sophia!"

Sophia smiled. You could tell she was feeling proud of her hard work.

"It's pretty good," Melissa G. agreed, "but, Molly, I know your costume is going to be great, too. We'll be the most beautiful princesses at the festival!"

Melissa G. and Molly both decided to be princesses. That was not surprising at all. They both love princess everything. Princess dolls. Princess dresses. Princess castles. They even had princess sunglasses with crown jewels on them. (Secretly I always wished I could have princess sunglasses, too, but I would never tell Melissa G. that. I don't want her to think I'm jealous or something when I'm really not!)

Melissa G. dragged Molly to the other side of the art room.

"Come on, Molly . . . I want to show you the silk scarf I attached to my crown. Now it looks just like a veil! I'll show you how to do it . . . It'll look so great! I know we're going to win the contest!"

Then they sat at an empty table on the other side of the art room. Melissa G. pulled out her costume—she was the princess from the book *The Princess and the Pea*. Molly was supposed to be her younger sister. I never knew that the princess had a younger sister, but Melissa G. insisted she could have one if she wanted to. Molly just went along with it—like she always does.

But today, Molly looked a little sad staring back at our table. Which is strange, since I thought Molly would like to be a princess. That's why she's perfect-match friends with Melissa G. I felt bad for Molly, but we had work to do!

"Okay, Sophia, what's left?" I asked.

"I just need to make the Lion's tail," continued Sophia.

"Yes . . . let's see what we can do about that," added Mr. Colón. "Oh, I bet we could make something out of these old jump ropes we have in the back supply closet . . . Come this way."

Mr. Colón grabbed Sophia's costume and headed to the back of the room to look for jump ropes. Sophia followed him. I pulled out my costume and started gluing feathers to my White Witch dress. It was looking very feathery. Sophia returned with what looked like a jump rope tail!

"Ha-ha!" I said. "Look at your tail!"

"I know," Sophia replied. "I'm almost done. I just need some yellow and orange yarn to make the tail fluffy at the end."

Sophia left her costume on the table next to me and went to go find some yarn. I continued adding feathers to my dress.

All of a sudden, everyone turned to the front of the room and started giggling.

It was Javier. He walked into the class with his costume on and he looked amazing. He was wearing a huge cardboard box that had a hole on top for his head and two holes on the sides for his arms. The box was painted dark blue with a light blue trim. He looked just like a wardrobe! It even had two doors in front that opened and closed!

"Javier!!" I screamed with delight as I ran over to him near the front of the classroom. "That is the best costume ever!! It's amazing!"

"Wow! That's so cool," said Adrian. Everyone started crowding around Javier. Mr. Colón and Sophia walked over, too.

"Javier, this is an excellent costume," said Mr. Colón as he inspected the cardboard box.

"Thanks," said Javier with a huge grin.

"I think you and your team have a real shot at winning the grand prize," Mr. Colón went on. "And, boy, this whole class is looking good. Looks like we have lots of winners here. I'd say there's a good chance Miss Thompson's class will win the most categories and become the winners of the pizza party! P.S. 387 is going to be the most creative school on Halloween!"

All the kids started patting Javier on the back—well, on the back of his wardrobe box! He had a big smile on his face.

"Thanks, Javier," said Adrian. "I can't wait for our pizza party next week! P.S. 387 rules!"

"No problem," said Javier, trying to play it cool.

"Javier, do you know what this means?" I yelled in a not-cool way. "Forget about the pizza party, we're gonna win the grand prize! We can finally get your spy kit from Mr. Magee's Toy Store! And that way we can solve more cases . . . do more news reports . . . and be even more famous!"

I couldn't think of anything more exciting. The school would be so proud of us. Plus a pizza party! This was gonna be the best Halloween ever.

Then it happened.

"Aaaahhhhhh!"

It was Sophia. She was screaming. It was such a loud screech, it gave me goose bumps on my arms.

"Sophia, what's wrong?" I asked her.

"My Lion costume is gone!"

CHAPTER
FOUR

The Hunt for a
Costume Crook

OKAY, okay, Sophia. Calm down. It must be here somewhere. We'll find it," said Mr. Colón.

Sophia looked like she was going to cry.

"Has anyone seen Sophia's costume?" Mr. Colón asked the class. Everyone shrugged.

"Well, I suggest you all help us look for it. Without Sophia's costume, this class may not win the pizza party . . ."

After that, the whole class started searching.

Mr. Colón checked the back closet to make sure no one had brought it there by accident. Sophia and I looked under our table, and Javier tried to help us but he was stuck. His wardrobe costume was not very easy to move around in.

"Uh . . . Emma . . . I can't really bend down on the floor."

"That's okay," I told him. "Why don't you just stand in the front of the room and look around? Let me know if you see anything suspicious."

"All right, got it," said Javier. He waddled to a spot near the door and called, "I'll be right here if you need me!"

"Okay!" I called back.

Sophia and I looked under every table and in every corner, but we couldn't find the Lion costume anywhere.

"This is so strange," said Mr. Colón. "How can a costume just disappear?"

"This is awful!" cried Sophia. "I worked so hard on that Lion outfit and now it's gone!"

"Now don't worry. We'll find it, I'm sure," Mr. Colón assured her.

"But Mr. Colón," I said, "we need to find it before the festival on Saturday. If we don't, we'll lose the contest!"

Then Sophia really started to cry.

Mr. Colón started asking each of the kids if they'd seen the costume. But I knew what we had to do.

"Sophia, come here," I said in a whisper.

I tugged at her sleeve and pulled her away to the front of the room. We walked over to Javier and huddled together, and I pulled out my camera phone and my Emma microphone.

"Guys, this is it," I said. "This is our next news story. If we work together we can figure out who took Sophia's costume. I know we can. But we have to hurry. We only have two days before the festival."

"Great idea," said Javier.

"I don't know," said Sophia, still sniffling. "How are we going to find it in two days?" Sophia was so sad that she was ready to give up. And that wasn't like her at all. Sophia is usually the one who tells *me* to never give up!

"Sophia, we can do it. Look—I'm a famous reporter. I'm good at this. And the three of us are like a team."

"Yeah!" said Javier.

"We can work on this together," I continued. "And, hey, then we'll all be famous. And we'll find your costume. And we'll win the contest!"

"Okay," said Sophia with a little smile.

"Okay, good," I said. "Now, Javier, did you notice anything suspicious while you were watching the class?"

"Not really. Well, I don't know . . . I kinda saw something, but I don't want you to get mad."

"Get mad about what?" asked Sophia.

"Well, it's not really suspicious . . . but I was looking at Melissa G. . . . and she was the only one who wasn't helping search for the costume. Melissa *and* Molly. They were just standing by their table. And it looked like Melissa G. was smiling."

"She was smiling?" I asked.

"Yeah. Like when Sophia started crying, it almost looked like Melissa G. was laughing."

"What??" I asked in amazement. That did it. Now I really was getting mad. Melissa G. might think she can push Molly around, but now she'd gone too far.

"She's so . . . she's just so . . . she's just so mean!" I yelled.

"It's okay, Emma," said Sophia. "Just ignore her. We don't care what she thinks anyway."

Then I thought of something.

"But, Sophia, we do care what she thinks." I turned on my camera phone. "Javier, I need you to tell us that again. But this time on camera!"

"Why?" Javier was confused.

"Don't you get it? Melissa G. took Sophia's costume! That's why she was smiling!" It seemed so obvious to me.

"But she just told Mr. Colón she hadn't seen the costume," said Sophia.

"Sophia, she's lying. I know she did it. Remember when she walked by and said she liked your costume?" I explained.

"Yeah?" Sophia said.

"Well, there you go."

"What do you mean? She said she liked it." Sophia was confused, too.

"I know she *said* she liked it. But I think she

was really just jealous. So she took the costume to make sure we didn't win the contest."

"You really think she would do that?" asked Javier.

"I know she would! We just have to prove it. And this is our first clue!"

CHAPTER
FIVE

I Know Who Did It

WE set up the camera phone and Sophia helped me record the interview with Javier. He told us what he saw all over again. Then I opened my backpack and pulled out the rest of my reporting tools, including my purple reporter pad and my shiny feather pencil.

I turned to the next free page and wrote at the top: The Case of the Missing Costume. Then I wrote underneath:

Clue #1: Javier saw Melissa G. smiling
after Sophia's costume went missing.

Just then, I heard someone laugh. I looked up
and it was Melissa G.! Again! So I grabbed the
camera phone and pointed it in her direction. I
recorded video of her laughing as she showed
Molly her costume. She had on a beautiful blue
princess dress with lots of lace, bows, and bead-
ing. It even had a flowing skirt with light blue
shimmers and sparkles. And when she spun
around, the skirt twirled in the air.

I started feeling even more mad. Her costume
was awesome. And now that she'd stolen Sophia's
costume, she might actually win the contest!

Molly was sitting down, also wearing a
princess dress. But she just sat there with her
backpack on. She looked upset. *She's probably
mad at Melissa, too,* I thought.

"C'mon, Sophia. Let's go talk to Melissa G."

Sophia and I ran over. You know that reporters have to do things quickly. Sophia held the camera and I pointed my Emma microphone right at Melissa.

"Melissa!" I said.

"What do you want?" Melissa G. answered.

"I want to know what happened to Sophia's Lion costume!"

"I don't know! I already told Mr. Colón that I haven't seen it."

"But you said you liked it," I reminded her.

"Yeah, so? I said I liked it because I thought it was a good costume. Big deal."

"Well, maybe you liked it so much you were worried you were going to lose the contest. So you decided to steal Sophia's costume to make sure we wouldn't win!"

Melissa started to look upset. Like her feelings were hurt. I wasn't sure what to do.

"Listen, Melissa, we don't care if you took it," I said with a nicer voice. "Just give it back."

"But I didn't take it!" Melissa yelled back.

"Then who did?" Sophia chimed in.

"Um . . . Melissa didn't take it," Molly blurted.

"How do you know?" I asked.

"Um . . . Melissa *couldn't* have taken it," Molly explained. "She was in the bathroom putting on her princess dress when Sophia screamed. She wasn't here when the costume disappeared."

"That's right!" said Melissa, like she was suddenly remembering. "When I came back to the art room, everyone had already started searching. Molly had to tell me what happened because I didn't know."

"Really?" I asked.

"Yes, really," answered Melissa. "And besides, I don't care about that old Lion costume. I was too busy twirling. It doesn't matter to me if Sophia has her costume or not. I know I'm going to win the contest either way!"

And with that, Melissa G. twirled to the other side of the room and pretended to lie down on a stack of imaginary mattresses.

Javier was still standing in the front of the classroom—still stuck in his costume. Sophia and I walked back over and told him what happened.

"So Melissa didn't do it?" Javier said.

"Nope," said Sophia.

"That's what she *says*," I added. "I still think she had something to do with it."

"But Melissa G. couldn't have done it," Sophia insisted. "You heard Molly."

"I guess you're right," I agreed. But I still wasn't convinced. Something just didn't make sense. But I didn't have a good reason to suspect Melissa anymore, so I just wrote down what I did know in my reporter pad.

Clue #2: Molly says Melissa G. was in the bathroom when the costume went missing. Melissa couldn't have taken it.

"Okay, everyone. Class is over," said Mr. Colón. "Miss Thompson is here to take you to the lunchroom."

Mr. Colón walked over to Javier, Sophia, and me.

"Listen, Sophia, I know you're upset. But don't panic. Your costume is around here somewhere and we'll figure it out."

I looked at Sophia and whispered, "That's right—*we'll* figure it out." And we walked out the door for lunch.

CHAPTER
SIX

Cloudy Judgment

THAT night I told Papi about my latest news story at school.

"*Pobrecita Sophia*," he said in Spanish. Poor Sophia.

"Yeah, she's pretty upset. *Bendito*," I added. That means "poor thing."

Papi helped me set up my laptop computer to record another report.

I wrote my news story on my purple reporter pad. Then I adjusted the laptop so the camera

was pointing toward me. Once I saw myself on screen, I laughed. I love seeing myself on TV!

I looked into the computer screen again with a serious reporter face. That was better. As usual, I was wearing my green velvet reporter blazer and my chunky white pearl necklace. My chocolate-pudding Slinky curls were in just the right position around my face. I looked just like a real reporter and I was ready to go on the air. I clicked record and said, "This is Emma and I'm on the air!"

I decided not to sing the intro like I normally would. Even though it sounds funny and famous that way, this was a serious report and I knew I had to be more serious. Then I read the story I had written on my purple reporter pad:

"As some of you may have heard, Sophia's Lion costume was stolen from the art room today. She worked very hard on this costume and needs it back. If she doesn't get it back, Sophia can't compete in the costume contest. And neither can I. Or Javier. We were a group costume from *The Lion, the Witch, and the Wardrobe.* Without Sophia's costume, Miss Thompson's class will win fewer categories and that means we might not get the pizza party.

Also—P.S. 387 might not win the grand prize! Sophia's costume was really good. P.S. 387 has to win . . . So we have to find her costume!"

Then I pressed play to show the two interviews we did that day with Javier and Melissa G. Afterward, I explained the clues I had discovered so far. And then I wrapped up my report.

"The case continues tomorrow. Stay tuned. We will get to the bottom of this!"

"Nice job," said Papi as soon as I was finished.

"Thanks, Papi. We don't have much time. The contest is the day after tomorrow and Sophia doesn't have a costume! I know Melissa G. took it and I'm going to prove it at school tomorrow."

"But, Emma, it sounds like Melissa couldn't have done it. She wasn't even there when it went missing, right?"

"I know but . . . she's not nice at all, Papi. *Ella es muy mala.* She's so mean!"

"Okay, okay. But remember, when you're a reporter and a detective, you can't let your feelings about someone cloud your judgment."

"What do you mean, Papi?"

"I mean, just because you don't like Melissa G. doesn't mean she took the costume. That's called bias—when you judge someone based on feelings instead of facts."

"So you think I have bias?" That sounded like I had a disease.

"Yes, I think you're being a little biased. It's not fair to Melissa G. And it's not nice to accuse someone of something you know they didn't do. *Eso es mal.* That's wrong."

"Okay, Papi. I'm sorry."

"It's okay, honey. You're learning! So, based on the facts, what do you think about Melissa G.?

I want you to think about what you *know* for certain happened so far."

"Well, I know Melissa G. wasn't in the art room when Sophia's costume went missing. That's a fact. So I guess that means she didn't take it. But if Melissa G. didn't take it, then who did?"

Papi shrugged. "Sounds like you have to interview some more witnesses."

"Yes! You're right! Tomorrow I'm going to talk to Adrian. He was there when Javier walked into the room with his wardrobe costume. Maybe he saw something?"

"Great idea! Remember, a good reporter and detective keeps her mind open to all possibilities."

"Got it."

I said good night to Papi. Tomorrow I would solve the case for sure!

CHAPTER
SEVEN
Why Do Girls Do That?

SOPHIA and I sat together on the school bus the next morning. She was so sad, she barely said a word. She just stared out the window.

"Is Sophia okay?" asked Molly. She was sitting across from us on the bus.

"No, Molly, she's not okay. But she will be. I'll make sure of that. I have to find out who took her costume. Today's the day to solve the case."

"Good luck," said Molly. "I really hope you find it. I would feel awful if someone took my costume."

"Thanks, Molly," I replied as the bus pulled up to our school. I stood up to get out. Sophia just sat there. "Come on, Sophia," I called. "We're here. Time to go."

"Oh, right. Thanks," she said as she slowly got out of her seat. She was even walking in a sad way. I waited so Sophia could go in front of me. Then I followed her down the aisle of the bus and Molly followed behind me. We all got off the bus and went into class.

"Okay, boys and girls, have a seat," said Miss Thompson. "Today we have a special visitor for our science lesson. Mr. Williams here has come all the way from the Bronx Zoo to introduce us to his special friend, Isadora the iguana."

Everyone got excited and stretched their necks to get a peek at the iguana. It was green and scaly like a lizard . . . but it was bigger.

"Hello, class. My name is Milo Williams . . . and I'd like you to meet Isadora." Mr. Williams held Isadora up so all of us could see her better. "Isadora the iguana is a baby. She's only three months old. She may look big now, but when she grows up, she'll be more than six feet long!"

"Whoa . . ." we all said. The iguana lesson was so interesting, even Sophia looked like she was having fun. I almost forgot I had a mystery to solve! Mr. Williams said everyone could have a turn to pet Isadora the iguana. I made sure to get behind Adrian at the end of the line.

"Hey, Adrian," I whispered with my camera phone and microphone in hand. But he didn't respond. He was busy watching people pet Isadora.

"Adrian!" I called a little bit louder. Then he turned around.

"What?"

"I need to interview you for my news story. I'm trying to find out who took Sophia's costume in the art room yesterday."

"Oh, cool. I'll be on TV!"

"Yup," I said. Then Adrian had to step forward. The line was moving. I didn't have much time, so I stepped forward with him and pressed record right away.

"Adrian, did you see who took Sophia's costume yesterday?"

"No, I didn't. I saw the costume on your art table. And then Javier walked in and his closet-box costume was so awesome, I walked over to him to see it."

"You mean his wardrobe costume," I corrected.

"Yeah, right. The box. I even knocked on his cardboard door to make sure it was real!"

"You did?"

"Uh-huh . . . I thought it was funny. But Ayana didn't think so, and pushed me! She pushed me so hard, I fell against the table."

"Which table?" I asked.

"Actually, your table. The table where you and Sophia were working."

"The table with the Lion costume on it??" I asked with excitement.

"Um . . . yeah. You know what, I had to grab on to it to hold my balance. I think some stuff fell off. I was going to pick it up but I had to go back over to Ayana and yell at her for pushing me! She shouldn't have pushed me! You know? Why do girls do that?"

"Okay . . . but do you think you knocked the costume off the table?"

"I'm not sure, but I probably did. I think I knocked everything off the table."

Then Adrian had to step forward again. We were almost at the front of the line.

"Hmm. Okay, thanks, Adrian." And then it was Adrian's turn and he moved forward to pet Isadora. I put my camera and Emma microphone away.

So Adrian knocked the costume onto the floor. But we looked on the floor and the costume wasn't there. Someone must have picked it up before we started looking.

It was my turn to pet Isadora. I reached out to touch her scaly back. She felt so strange. But she was also more beautiful than I had thought.

I realized sometimes things aren't always what they seem.

Someone took the Lion costume after Adrian knocked it on the floor. Now I just had to figure out one thing—who?

CHAPTER EIGHT

Anonymous Tip

AFTER everyone had a turn to pet Isadora the iguana, Mr. Williams put her back in her cage and said good-bye.

The rest of the morning we did independent reading and practiced our spelling words. Finally, at lunch, I sat down with Sophia and Javier in the cafeteria. Shakira and Lizzie sat with us, too.

"Emma, I saw your report last night. I can't believe Sophia's costume is gone!" said Shakira.

Sophia just sulked.

"I know, but I'm making progress on the case," I said, then added, turning to Sophia, "We're gonna find the costume. I promise."

"Forget it, Emma. It's no use." Sophia sighed. "I've decided not to go to the Halloween Festival anyway."

"But you love Halloween!" cried Lizzie.

"Yeah, don't give up now," encouraged Javier. "I know Emma will figure out what happened. Right, Emma?"

"Well . . . I'm trying. And I have a new clue." I told them about what Adrian said in class this morning.

"Oh, yeah," said Javier. "I remember Adrian knocking on my box. I didn't care, but Ayana sure did. She's always pushing Adrian around and arguing with him one minute, and then asking him to play at recess the next minute. Girls are weird."

"See that!" said Lizzie. "We just have to figure out who picked the costume up after Adrian pushed it on the floor."

"That's right," I agreed. Then I opened my backpack to get my purple reporter pad and shiny feather pencil so I could write down the latest clue. When I reached into the side pocket of my backpack, I felt a piece of paper. That was odd. I didn't put a piece of paper in there. I pulled everything out. And there it was. Next to my reporter pad was a note.

"Guys, look at this!" I showed them.

"Read it!" demanded Lizzie.

I read the note out loud. Here's what it said:

I know what happened to the Lion costume. Someone took it. Check Sophia's desk in Miss Thompson's class.

That was it. The person who wrote the note didn't sign their name. It was an anonymous tip!

Sophia looked up.

"My desk? But I was at my desk this morning. I didn't see the costume there."

"Hmm. What does this mean?" I wondered.

"Whoever wrote that note knows what happened," said Javier. "We have to check Sophia's desk again. Sophia, maybe you just didn't see it in there this morning?"

"Javier, it's my costume. I love it. I know I would've seen it if it was in my desk," insisted Sophia.

"Well, what if it was in your desk," continued Javier, "but someone covered it with a magic invisible blanket? Yeah . . . So it was there but it was invisible, so you just couldn't see it!"

We all rolled our eyes.

"Sure, Javier. Sure," I said. "Sophia, as soon as lunch is over, let's ask permission to go to the library instead of recess. But on our way to the library, let's check your desk one more time. Okay?"

"Okay," said Sophia nervously.

"Me too. I'm coming, too!" insisted Javier. "I have to see how this invisible blanket really works . . ."

"Javier! There is no invisible blanket! Come on, Sophia, let's go ask Geraldine the lunch lady if we can go to the library," I said.

"Okay, Emma. I'm sure my costume's not there, but we might as well look. See you later, Lizzie. Bye, Shakira."

"Bye, guys! Good luck!" they called back.

And off we went to find Geraldine. Javier followed behind.

CHAPTER
NINE

There's No Such Thing as an Invisible Blanket!

GERALDINE said we could go to the library, so we started walking in that direction. Then instead of turning down the hall to the library, we went up the stairs toward our classroom.

"Okay, let's hurry before we get caught," I said nervously.

We ran over to Sophia's desk and lifted the top to look inside.

"See, I told you guys the costume wasn't here." Sophia looked disappointed.

"You haven't even checked under the invisible blanket yet. Of course we can't see it," said Javier. He wasn't even joking.

Sophia and Javier started arguing about invisible blankets again. But I noticed something stuck in the hinge of the desk top. I had to get a closer look, so I moved past Sophia and Javier. I bent over to inspect the lid. And then I found it. There was a small orange strip of felt.

"Hey, guys! Look!!" I screamed.

"What?" they both asked.

"This . . ." I pulled the felt strip loose from the hinge and held it up. "Look familiar, Sophia?"

"What? Is that part of the invisible blanket?" asked Javier.

"Wait—that strip of felt is from my Lion's mane!" said Sophia.

"Yes!" I cried. "It must have gotten stuck in the hinge and fallen off. That means your costume was here. The person who wrote the anonymous note was right."

"But it's not here now," Sophia sighed. "Where is it?"

"I don't know. But, Sophia, we're getting closer!"

"Emma, we have to find out who wrote that anonymous note," said Sophia. "He or she probably knows something more." She was starting to sound hopeful.

"You're right. But how are we going to figure out who wrote it?"

"Well . . . let's see." Sophia examined the note. "It's written with pink ink. Maybe we can figure out who's been using a pink pen . . ."

"Yes! As soon as everyone gets back to class, we'll look at their pens," I suggested.

"Uh, guys . . ." said Javier.

"What is it?" we asked.

"I think I hear something. We should really go."

"I know, I know. We will," I told him. "I just have to write these clues down in my reporter pad."

I pulled out my pad and wrote:

Clue #3: Adrian knocked the costume onto the floor.

Clue #4: Anonymous note written in pink ink told us to look on Sophia's desk.

Clue #5: We found an orange felt strip in Sophia's desk. Costume was here, but is gone now.

"No really," Javier said again, sounding nervous. "We need to leave."

"Okay, I'm done. Let's go," I said as we ran toward the door. I quickly put my purple reporter pad and shiny feather pencil back in my backpack. I put the piece of felt in the side pocket.

"Someone's coming!" Javier gasped. We stopped in our tracks before we got to the door.

"It's too late. Someone's here."

CHAPTER
TEN

Check with Charlie

SOPHIA, Javier, and I hurried over to the coat closet to hide. Just as we closed the closet doors behind us, Miss Thompson walked into the classroom with Mr. Colón.

"I don't know what happened," we heard Mr. Colón say as we peeked through a crack in the doors. "One minute the costume was there, the next it was gone. We've looked everywhere and so far it hasn't turned up."

"Did you ask Melissa G.?" asked Miss Thompson. "I know those girls don't always get

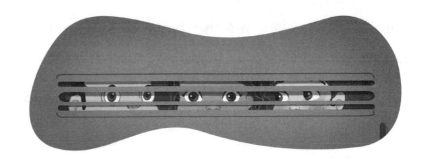

along. I don't think she would steal a costume—
but you never know."

I knew it! I knew Melissa G. had something
to do with it. And Miss Thompson thought
so, too!

"I thought about that, too. But Melissa was
not there when it happened. I gave her permission to use the bathroom. I was holding
the costume myself when she walked out of the
room. And I saw her walk back in after the costume went missing. It definitely wasn't her."

Sophia and I looked at each other and
shrugged. I guess it wasn't Melissa G. after all.
I felt bad for blaming her. Papi was right. I

should've checked all the facts before making assumptions.

"I know," Miss Thompson said. "Have you checked with Charlie the custodian? He might know something."

"Actually, I haven't. Great idea. I'll do that after school today," answered Mr. Colón.

Miss Thompson grabbed a folder and what looked like her own lunch bag. Then they both walked out of the classroom. We waited a minute after they left and then we opened the closet doors and stepped out.

"That *is* a great idea." I said. "I bet Charlie the custodian knows something."

"I know exactly where he is, too," said Sophia. "Come on, let's go there now."

The three of us snuck out of the classroom. We looked both ways to make sure no one saw us. Then we raced back to the lunchroom. All the kids were outside playing. Charlie the custodian was mopping up in the back. We started running in his direction.

"Emma!" someone suddenly called. We stopped in our tracks and turned around. It was Geraldine the lunch lady walking right toward us. "You know you're not supposed to run in here! I thought you three were going to the library?" she asked. I could tell we were in trouble.

"Oh, um . . . yeah, we were," I said. But I didn't know what to say next.

"So why aren't you there now?" Geraldine wanted to know. Sophia and I just looked at each other nervously. I stared at my feet. Then Javier started talking.

"Geraldine, they didn't really want to go to the library," he said.

"Is that so?" she asked with her hands on her hips.

"Yeah . . . I tricked the girls into going with me by telling them I had seen an invisible blanket in the library. But it's not actually there. I made it up. They left and insisted on coming back to join the class in the school yard."

Geraldine the lunch lady started giving Javier a lecture about how invisible blankets aren't real, and even if they were real, you can't go around searching for them during lunchtime.

"You girls go along. Javier, you come with me. You earned fifteen minutes on the bench." Geraldine pulled Javier outside to sit on the bench while the other kids played. He winked at us as he left the lunchroom. I felt awful that Javier got in trouble. But we still had a case to solve, so Sophia and I ran to talk to Charlie the custodian. He was still mopping in the back.

"Hey, girls, what's your hurry? Why are you running on this wet floor? You know you could get hurt," Charlie said.

"Oh, sorry, Charlie," we said together.

"Charlie," Sophia began, "I lost my Aslan the Lion costume I was making for Halloween. We were hoping you might have seen it?"

Charlie began to open his mouth to reply but then I shouted, "Wait! Don't answer that. Not yet." I hurriedly grabbed the camera phone and microphone and pressed record. "Okay, now. Now you can answer."

"Is that a camera?" Charlie asked.

"Yes, this is a story for 'Emma Is On the Air.' We're trying to figure out who took Sophia's Aslan costume."

"All right, then," he agreed. "As a matter of fact, Sophia, I did see your costume."

Sophia and I looked at each other and smiled.

"Where??" Sophia asked.

"It was right on top of one of the desks in Miss Thompson's classroom. I saw it there yesterday. I figured I'd better move it because that night they were going to use that classroom for adult school. English lessons, I think."

"So you moved the costume?" I asked. "Do you remember where you put it?"

"I wasn't sure who it belonged to. I thought it might belong to that little girl Molly, because I saw her with the costume earlier in the day, but I wasn't sure. It looked important, so I put it in the lost and found bin and figured Molly could find it there the next day if it really was hers."

Suddenly we heard a whistle blow from outside. All the kids started lining up to head back to class. Lunch was over.

"The lost and found bin! That's great! Thanks, Charlie!" I called.

"Anytime, girls!" Charlie replied as he continued to mop the floor.

Sophia and I put the camera away as all the kids started walking back into the lunchroom—including Javier.

We ran over to Javier and told him what happened.

"That's great!" he said.

"Oh, I hope he's right. I hope my costume's there," said Sophia. We made plans to head straight to the lost and found bin after school.

"But, guys, Charlie said he saw Molly with

the costume. Why would Molly have Sophia's costume?" I wondered.

"He must be confused," Sophia said. "He wasn't sure who he saw. He probably saw me holding the costume, not Molly. Molly would never take my costume." Sophia seemed pretty convinced.

"Yeah, you're right. Molly wouldn't do that," I agreed. "Oh, and Javier, sorry you got benched."

"Yeah, I'm sorry you got in trouble, Javier," Sophia added.

"Eh. That's no problem. I get benched all the time. The bench is my good friend, it's no big deal."

Javier is the best. I pulled out my reporter pad and wrote down:

Clue #6: Charlie the custodian says he put the costume in the lost and found bin.

This case was about to get solved!

CHAPTER ELEVEN

Lost and Found

WE had to wait until after school was over to check for Sophia's costume. Sophia, Javier, and I lined up in the front hallway with everyone else for the school bus. When no one was looking, we snuck into the back lunchroom door and headed straight for the lost and found bin.

"Look inside, Sophia," I said.

"Okay, here I go . . ." she said as she opened the lid to the bin. Sophia sifted through the clothes. Then she started throwing clothes out of the bin and up into the air. A green winter hat landed perfectly on Javier's head!

"Awesome. Thanks," Javier joked. But Sophia wasn't laughing.

"I can't find it!" Sophia called from inside the bin. She was digging so deep, her feet were dangling off the floor. "It's not here," she said, standing up with a sigh.

"Are you sure?" I asked.

"Yeah. I looked at everything in there. It's not here."

"I'm sorry, Sophia," I said, and put my arm around her. But Javier wouldn't give up that easily. He started looking in the bin, too.

"Javier's right," I said. "We can't give up yet. Let's think. We know Charlie the custodian put the costume in the bin . . . Who might have taken it out?"

"I don't know. I'm tired. Let's just go." Sophia was getting sad again.

Then Javier started sneezing.

"Aaachoo!" he sneezed again.

"Okay, let's go get on the bus," I agreed. "Come on, Javier."

We all left to get on the bus. Sophia looked really sad. And I felt sad for her. We plunked down into our regular seats and rode home. No one said a word to each other. The Halloween Festival was the next day, and Sophia didn't have a costume.

"Well, Sophia, I'm not giving up yet, but maybe you can figure out another costume to wear to the festival, just in case we don't find Aslan the Lion," I suggested as the bus ran over a bumpy part of the street.

"My mom said I could wear my big sister's costume from two Halloweens ago. She was dressed up as a chocolate chip cookie," Sophia replied.

"That's a great idea! You should wear that, Sophia."

"It's a funny costume, but it's not from a book. And I didn't make it. I won't be able to enter the costume contest."

"Oh. Right."

"I'm sorry, Emma," Sophia said as the bus pulled over to our stop. "We're not going to win the contest and it's all my fault."

"Don't say that," I said. "It's not your fault at all. And it's not over yet."

"I'll see you at the festival tomorrow. Bye, Emma."

Sophia hurried off the bus to meet her mom and walk home.

This was awful. Once I got home, I wrote down the last clue in my reporter pad.

#7: The costume was not in the lost and found bin.

I still had a news report to do. This was a tough case, but it wasn't over yet. When you're a famous reporter and detective, you can't just give up. So I headed upstairs to my computer and recorded my last news report before the festival.

"Hello, everyone," I began. "This is Emma and I'm on the air! As you know we've been trying to find Sophia's missing Lion costume . . ."

I told them all about my interview with Adrian. About the secret anonymous note with pink ink. About the strip of orange felt. About the interview with Charlie the custodian. And finally I told them that the costume was not in the lost and found bin.

"So that's it. We still can't find the costume.

Sophia is going to have wear her big sister's old costume. And that means no contest. But it's not over yet. 'Emma Is On the Air' . . . is still on the case! Stayed tuned."

And with that I closed my laptop and wondered how I was going to find Sophia's costume.

CHAPTER TWELVE

¡La Bruja Blanca!

THE next day, we all got dressed up for the festival. My White Witch costume was amazing. My white dress was covered in white feathers and sparkly sequins. We cut up the bottom of the dress into shredded strips. Then I had my fur shaggy rug coat, my magic wand, and my tinfoil ice crown!

"¡La Bruja Blanca!" Papi said with a smile when I walked into the living room. *"¡Fantástico!"*

"Thanks, Papi! I think I do look pretty fantastic! And so do you!" Papi had on a Batman mask.

"Gracias, mi *Bruja Blanca.*"

Mom was wearing a Catwoman mask, and baby Mia was dressed as baby Supergirl. They were having a superhero Halloween.

Even my cat, Luna, got to go! Of course, she was my witch's black cat. Except Luna's fur is brown, not black. And the White Witch didn't have a cat, according to my mom. But I thought the White Witch would probably really like a brown cat. Plus I was still looking for Sophia's costume and I needed my reporter's assistant by my side! Mom agreed, as long as Luna stayed on a leash and we brought her kitty bag in case she got scared.

We walked into the gymnasium at my school and it looked so spooky. There were Halloween decorations everywhere. Orange and black streamers and balloons hung from the ceiling. There was a haunted house bouncy castle.

There was a table with gross food that felt like brains and eyeballs!! And there was music blasting over a dance floor where kids in spooky costumes were dancing.

Everyone was laughing and screaming and dancing. Everyone except Sophia. Sophia was sitting in the corner. She was the saddest chocolate chip cookie I'd ever seen. I walked right over to her.

"Hey, nice cookie! You look delicious!" I joked.

Sophia barely smiled. "Hi, Emma."

"Aw, cheer up, Sophia. It's still a really fun party. And look who I brought?" I showed her how I had Luna in her cat bag. Sophia instantly started to smile.

"Luna! Hi, kitty!" Sophia loves Luna. We took her out of the cat bag so Sophia could pet her. Then we heard a voice on the loudspeaker.

"Okay, boys and girls!" It was Principal Lee. She was speaking into the DJ's microphone. "Welcome to the Washington Heights Halloween Festival!"

Everyone started cheering and clapping.

"We're so happy to have you all here at our wonderful school today. You all look so spooky! I'm glad you came in such creative costumes. Our literary costume contest will begin in one hour. Come back to the dance floor at four p.m. if you think you can win! Enjoy."

Everyone started clapping again. Sophia and I looked at each other and sighed. We knew we wouldn't be winning that contest. Bye-bye, spy kit. We probably wouldn't win the pizza party for Miss Thompson's class, either. Without Sophia, our class would have a hard time winning the most categories.

I spotted Melissa G. across the dance floor. She looked so beautiful. She'd probably win the contest now, I thought. Then she headed right in our direction. She looked worried.

"Hi, Emma, hi, Sophia. Have you guys seen Molly anywhere?" asked Melissa G.

"Hi, Melissa. I haven't seen her," answered Sophia. "I've been here awhile. No sign of her."

"I can't find her. She was supposed to meet me here half an hour ago. We're both supposed to be princesses together." Melissa G. looked sad and worried.

"Maybe she's in the bounce house? It's hard to see inside," I offered. I know I don't like Melissa G., but I felt bad for her.

"Thanks, Emma." Melissa G. walked off toward the spooky bounce house. As we watched her walk away, I spotted a piece of blue furniture in the corner. Just sitting there. Not moving an inch. I knew that piece of furniture right away! I grabbed Sophia and we headed right over. Sophia still had Luna in her arms.

"Hi!" I said with a giggle. The furniture said nothing at first. So I knocked on the two front doors.

"Who's there?" a muffled voice asked.

"It's me, Emma."

"And Sophia!" She giggled.

Then a head popped up on top.

"Oh, hi, Emma! Hi, Sophia!" Javier said back with a smile. We all laughed.

"Javier, your wardrobe costume is so cool. I love it," I told him.

"Thanks," he said. Then Javier let out a big sneeze. Then another one.

"Achooo!" he roared.

"Bless you!" I said back.

"Who's that?" Javier asked, pointing to Luna.

"Oh, this is my cat, Luna. She's my brown witch's cat and my reporter's assistant. She's part of my costume."

Javier sneezed again.

"Hi, Luna—achoo!" he said as he covered his mouth with his hand.

"Javier, why are you sneezing so much?" I wondered.

"Oh . . . I'm allergic to cats," he replied. And then he sneezed again.

"You're allergic to cats?" I asked. Javier answered with another sneeze.

"You're allergic to CATS!!" Sophia said with excitement.

"Yes. I just told you that. *Achooo!*"

"Emma, that's it!" Sophia said. "I know

exactly where my costume is! Come on, guys, we have to go! Hurry!"

"Ok. Achoo! Where are we going? Achoo!"

"We're going to the lost and found bin!" Sophia answered. And she just started running. We had no choice but to run after her.

CHAPTER
THIRTEEN

Allergies and Answers

BUT, Sophia, we looked in the lost and found bin. The costume isn't there," I reminded her.

"I know. But we have to look again. Come on. Hurry!"

Then Sophia stopped and looked down at Luna.

"Here, Emma. Take Luna and give her back to your mom and dad. We don't need to torture Javier any longer."

"Okay," I said. I ran over and handed Luna to Papi. I told them we had another clue and we'd be right back. Then I ran back to Sophia and Javier and we raced as fast as we could to the lost and found. Now that Luna was gone, Javier finally stopped sneezing.

"Sophia, I still don't understand what we're doing here," I said.

"Yeah, we know it's not here," agreed Javier.

"Javier. Have you noticed that you stopped sneezing?" Sophia asked him.

"Um . . . yeah," he replied. "Luna is with Emma's *papi*. Now I'm fine."

"Okay, now do me a favor. Look inside the lost and found bin," Sophia instructed.

"But, Sophia . . . I already looked here."

"I know you did. Just please look again."

Javier agreed. He took off his wardrobe costume and dug inside. Then it happened.

"Achoo!" he sneezed.

"I knew it," Sophia said with a smile.

"Knew what?" Javier asked as he lifted his head out of the bin.

"The costume *has* to be here. Emma and I glued some of Luna's cat fur to the Lion costume. That's why you sneezed in the lost and found bin yesterday. That's why you sneezed just now. The costume has to be here!"

"Sophia! You're so smart!! Of course!" I screamed.

Then I started digging through the bin with Javier and Sophia. We all dug and dug but still couldn't find it.

"Wait—I have an idea." Javier said. He lifted the lost and found bin up and pulled it out from the corner it was sitting in. And what do you know? There it was. Sophia's Lion costume.

"Found it!" Javier proclaimed as he held the costume up over his head.

"Javier!!!" I screamed. "You did it!!"

"Yup! *Achoo*! Just had to look *behind* the bin."

I pulled out my camera phone that I had hidden inside my costume. You know, just in case. I shot video of Javier holding the costume.

"I love looking behind things," he continued. "*Achoo*! Here, Sophia, you take this." Javier handed the costume over and took a deep breath.

"That's better. Look what else was under the lost and found—a blue-striped glove. Nice. It'll go perfect inside my wardrobe doors . . ."

Javier started searching for more things to add to his costume.

But Sophia and I ran.

"Sophia, you go to the bathroom and put on that Lion costume! I have to go to the computer lab and let everyone know we solved the case!"

"Okay," she agreed. And we split up. There wasn't much time before the contest began, so we had to hurry.

CHAPTER
FOURTEEN

The Last Report

THE computer lab was empty when I got there. Which was perfect because I didn't have time to talk. It was 3:45 and Sophia only had fifteen minutes to put on her costume, and enter the contest!

I sat at my usual computer and set it up to record my report. I was still in my White Witch costume instead of my professional reporter blazer. But there was no time to go home and change. This would have to do.

"Hello, everyone, and happy Halloween!" I said as I looked into the camera. Everything was ready to go. I didn't have time to write a script down on paper, so I just wrote the script in my head and hoped I would remember it all.

"This is Emma and I'm on the air," I continued. "We solved the case! It turns out Charlie the custodian was right. The Aslan the Lion costume was in the lost and found bin after all! Sophia, Javier, and I just found it there—it was stuck behind the bin!"

I showed everyone the video of Javier holding the costume. Then I explained about Luna and the sneezing and Javier's cat allergy.

"I still haven't figured out who took the costume from the floor after Adrian knocked it off the table. But it doesn't matter. We found it! We're about to enter the contest. And win for P.S. 387."

Then I said, "Thanks for watching 'Emma Is On the Air.' See you next time."

I ran back to the gymnasium to find Sophia and Javier.

"Two minutes!" Principal Lee said into the loudspeaker. "Anyone entering the costume contest should be behind the dance floor in two minutes."

There was no time left. I found Javier by the snack table eating eyeball gum balls. I grabbed him by the door handle and pulled him to the edge of the dance floor. We waited there—but no sign of Sophia.

"Okay, everyone . . . the Washington Heights Halloween Festival costume contest is about to begin . . ."

Still nothing.

"Emma, where is Sophia?" Javier asked, clearly nervous.

"She's getting ready," I assured him. "She'll be here any second."

The contest began and the first people entered the dance floor in their costumes. I was getting nervous, too. And then I saw her.

"Look! Here she comes." I pointed. "And she's not alone. She's with Molly."

"Molly?" Javier asked, confused.

"Sophia, you look so great!" I told her as she and Molly walked over to us. The Lion's mane was so colorful and bright. She looked just like Aslan.

"Thanks!" she answered.

"Hi, Molly!" I said. "Melissa's been looking all over for you." And then I noticed it. Molly was not dressed as a princess. She was Roo from *Winnie-the-Pooh*!! But before I could ask her about her costume, we heard our names called. Javier, Sophia, and I ran onto the dance floor.

"Okay, our next contestants have arrived," said Principal Lee into the microphone. "This is a group costume. We have Aslan the Lion, the White Witch, and the wardrobe from the book *The Lion, the Witch, and the Wardrobe.*"

Everyone started cheering as we walked across the dance floor. It felt great. I just knew we were gonna win. We walked back into the crowd so the next contestants could have a turn.

"We did it!" I shouted.

"Really think we're going to win?" Sophia asked.

"I hope so!" I answered.

Then it was Molly's turn. She strutted down the dance floor—proud as can be in her Roo costume.

"Hey, Sophia," I whispered. "What's up with Molly's costume? Why were you walking in with her? Looks like she stood up to Melissa after all."

"Yeah, I guess she did," Sophia replied. "I saw her walking in the front door when I was coming out of the bathroom. She said she saw your news report and rushed right over to make it into the costume contest. I wasn't sure why—but there was no time to ask. We had to run to get here in time."

"Hmm. That's strange."

When Molly was done showing her costume . . . Melissa G. ran over to her.

"Molly?? What are you doing? Where's your princess costume? You're supposed to be my little sister!"

"I decided not to wear it!" Molly said with a determined look on her face.

"But why? We were supposed to be beautiful princesses together—like always." Melissa looked confused.

"You know what, Melissa? I'm sick of being a princess all the time! Can't I just be something else for once?"

"I guess. If you want to," said Melissa G. Then it was Melissa's turn to show her costume, so she walked off, looking shocked. And maybe even sad. Molly just stood there. She looked happy! She walked right over to us.

"Wow, Molly—you look great!" I said. Sophia and Javier agreed.

"Thanks!" she said. "You were right. I decided I should be whatever I want to be. I made this costume when Melissa wasn't looking. I was still too scared to wear it. And then I saw your report, Emma. I was so happy you guys found the Lion costume, I decided I should wear my costume, too. So I rushed to school to enter the contest."

"Good for you," said Sophia.

Then I noticed something. Molly's costume looked a lot like Sophia's—just a kangaroo version. It had the same oval-shaped piece of felt sewn to the front to make the belly. Molly also had an extra piece of felt to make a pocket for the pouch. But she also wore a leotard and tights . . . and a tail made out of jump rope.

And just like that, a thought popped in my head. I knew what happened.

CHAPTER
FIFTEEN

Mystery Solved

HEY, Molly . . . how'd you get the idea to sew a felt oval patch on the front to make the belly?" I asked her.

"Oh . . . um. I just thought of it," Molly said.

"Because it looks a lot like the oval patch on my Lion costume . . ." Sophia realized.

"Yeah, um, I got the idea from you, Sophia."

"Charlie the custodian said he saw you holding Sophia's Lion costume the other day," Javier added. They figured out what I was thinking.

"Molly, did you take Sophia's costume?" I asked her.

Molly didn't say anything. She just stood there. And then she started to cry. I felt pretty bad. I didn't mean to make her cry.

"Molly, don't cry," I said.

"Yeah, don't cry," Sophia added. "I have the costume back now, so it's okay. I just want to know what happened."

"Okay. I'll tell you," Molly said as she tried to dry her tears with her hands. "I really wanted to be Roo for Halloween. But Melissa G. thought it was a baby costume. I didn't want her to know that I was gonna be Roo no matter what she said. But I needed help making my costume. Sophia, I saw your costume fall on the floor, so I picked it up. I was going to put it back on the art table, but then I decided to inspect it for a little while and see if I could figure out how you made it. It was just so good. I was going to put it back a couple minutes later, but then you screamed. You said it was missing and the whole class started looking for it. I didn't want everyone to know that I had taken it to learn how to make a Roo costume. Melissa might make fun of me. So I panicked. I stuffed your Lion costume in my backpack. Then after school that day I put it back on your desk. Honest. I thought you'd find it there the next day. I'm sorry. I didn't mean to ruin your Halloween."

Sophia took a deep breath and said, "That's okay. I know you didn't mean it. I wish you would've just told me, though. I never would've made fun of you."

"I know. You're right," Molly said. "I just got scared. I didn't know what to do. I felt so awful about it. I didn't even want to come to the festival because I felt so guilty. But then I saw you finally found it and I thought maybe everything would be okay after all."

"Is that why you wrote me an anonymous note?" I asked. I figured the note must have come from Molly. Who else knew where the costume was?

"What note?" Molly asked.

"The anonymous tip. It was written with pink ink. Do you have a pink pen?" I asked.

"No, I have blue and purple. I don't have pink. I don't know who wrote that note."

All of a sudden, we heard Principal Lee on the microphone.

"Boys and girls, we have the results of our costume contest."

"Okay, never mind, Molly." I let it go. We didn't have time to worry about that now anyway. The contest results were in. Everybody hurried to the dance floor to hear who won. Principal Lee started going through the categories one at a time. Lots of people won prizes. Javier won most original costume. I won most creative witch! Sophia won most artistic costume. Even Melissa G. won most beautiful princess costume. And Molly won best animal costume.

"Okay. Time to figure out which class won the most categories," announced Principal Lee. "Well, it looks like the kids from Mrs. Garcia's class from P.S. 525 have done extremely well. You won seven categories."

The kids from that class all screamed with applause.

"But look here. Miss Thompson's class right here at P.S. 387 has also done well. You won eight categories! You are the winners of the pizza party!"

We all started jumping and screaming so loudly, the grown-ups near us covered their ears.

"Congratulations, Miss Thompson's class. Settle down now. It's time to announce who won the overall award and the grand prize—a gift certificate at Mr. Magee's Toy Store."

This was it. This was the prize we really needed to win in order to get Javier his spy kit. Sophia, Javier, and I nervously held one another's hands.

"And the winner is . . ." said Principal Lee, "Justine Singer from P.S. 525. Come on up, Justine, and show everyone your costume again. Justine is Hedwig the owl from Harry Potter! Everyone give Justine a round of applause."

"Oh, no. We lost," I said.

"Well, we did win the pizza party," said Sophia.

"I know—and that's great—but now we can't buy Javier's spy kit." I was already making plans to go to Magee's. Now everything was ruined. I couldn't believe it.

"Emma, I don't think Javier's all that upset about it . . ." Sophia said with a giggle.

"What do you mean?"

"Look." Sophia pointed to the dance floor. And there was Javier in the middle, doing the robot dance from inside his wardrobe box. He looked so silly. But everyone started dancing around him.

"Come on . . ." said Sophia as she pulled my arm. And we went out there and started dancing, too.

I guess it wasn't so bad. We found Sophia's costume, we figured out who took it, and why . . . and we won a pizza party. I still didn't know

who sent that anonymous note. But I was sure I'd figure that out some day. In the meantime—I was still famous! And I started doing the famous jumpy dance in the middle of the dance floor.

"Woo-hoo!" said Javier. "Best Halloween ever."

And we danced all night long.

EMMA'S TIPS FOR NOT-BORING NEWS

1. **Run everywhere!** Real reporters need to get places fast. But don't <u>talk</u> too fast—then people might have to press the slow button and watch you in slow motion!

2. **Holiday news is not boring**—especially on Halloween, when you can do your news report in a costume! You can also dress up as a news reporter for Halloween. That way you're always ready to go on the air!

3. **Be nice!** Sometimes when people are mean to you, you might be tempted to do a news story about how not nice they are. Don't do it! Then <u>you</u> are the one who is not nice. Plus that's not <u>newsworthy</u>. Which means it's probably boring!

4. **Find a news team!** Reporting is much more fun when you do it with your friends. That way you can have a whole <u>team</u> finding clues and solving cases!

See you on the air!

Emma will be back ON THE AIR in

#3: SHOWTIME!